P9-DGP-999

🌷 A GOLDEN BOOK • NEW YORK

Compilation copyright © 2017 by Penguin Random House LLC.
All rights reserved. This 2017 edition was published in the United States by Golden Books, an imprint of Random House Children's Books,
a division of Penguin Random House LLC, 1745 Broadway, New York, NY 10019. Golden Books, A Golden Book,
A Little Golden Book, the G colophon, and the distinctive gold spine are registered trademarks
of Penguin Random House LLC. A Little Golden Book Classic is a trademark of Penguin Random House LLC.
Tootle and Tawny Scrawny Lion are trademarks of Penguin Random House LLC.
The works that appear herein were originally published separately as the following:
Tawny Scrawny Lion copyright © 1952, renewed 1980 by Penguin Random House LLC.
Tootle copyright © 1945, renewed 1973 by Penguin Random House LLC.
The Jolly Barnyard copyright © 1950, renewed 1978 by Penguin Random House LLC.
randomhousekids.com
Educators and librarians, for a variety of teaching tools, visit us at
RHTeachersLibrarians.com
ISBN 978-0-375-97608-7

This special edition was printed for Kohl's Department Stores, Inc.
(for distribution on behalf of Kohl's Cares, LLC, its wholly owned subsidiary)
by Random House Children's Books, a division of Penguin Random House LLC, New York.

KOHL'S
Style 97608
Factory Number 126509
Production Date 01/2017

Ages 3 and up

MANUFACTURED IN CHINA
10 9 8 7 6 5 4 3 2 1

Random House Children's Books supports the First Amendment and celebrates the right to read.

Tenggren's TAWNY SCRAWNY LION

by KATHRYN JACKSON
illustrated by GUSTAF TENGGREN

Once there was a tawny, scrawny, hungry
lion who never could get enough to eat.

He chased monkeys on Monday—

—kangaroos on Tuesday—

—zebras on Wednesday—

—bears on Thursday—

—camels on Friday—

and on Saturday, elephants!

And since he caught everything he ran after, that lion should have been as fat as butter. But he wasn't at all. The more he ate, the scrawnier and hungrier he grew.

The other animals didn't feel one bit safe. They stood at a distance and tried to talk things over with the tawny, scrawny lion.

"It's all your fault for running away," he grumbled. "If I didn't have to run, run, run for every single bite I get, I'd be fat as butter and

sleek as satin. Then I wouldn't have to eat so much, and you'd last longer!"

Just then, a fat little rabbit came hopping through the forest, picking berries. All the big animals looked at him and grinned slyly.

"Rabbit," they said. "Oh, you lucky rabbit! We appoint you to talk things over with the lion."

That made the little rabbit feel very proud.
"What shall I talk about?" he asked eagerly.
"Any old thing," said the big animals. "The
important thing is to go right up close."
So the fat little rabbit hopped right up to the
big hungry lion and counted his ribs.

"You look much too scrawny to talk things over,"
he said. "So how about supper at my house first?"

"What's for supper?" asked the lion.

The little rabbit said, "Carrot stew." That sounded awful to the lion. But the little rabbit said, "Yes sir, my five fat sisters and my four fat

brothers are making a delicious big carrot stew right now!"

"What are we waiting for?" cried the lion. And he went hopping away with the little rabbit, thinking of ten fat rabbits, and looking just as jolly as you please.

"Well," grinned all the big animals. "That should take care of Tawny-Scrawny for today."

Before very long, the lion began to wonder if
they would ever get to the rabbit's house.

First, the fat little rabbit kept stopping to pick
berries and mushrooms and all sorts of good-
smelling herbs. And when his basket was full,
what did he do but flop down on the river bank!

"Wait a bit," he said.

"I want to catch a few fish for the stew."
That was almost too much for the hungry lion.
For a moment, he thought he would have to eat
that one little rabbit then and there. But he
kept saying "five fat sisters and four fat brothers"
over and over to himself. And at last the two were
on their way again.

"Here we are!" said the rabbit, hopping around a turn with the lion close behind him. Sure enough, there was the rabbit's house, with a big pot of carrot stew bubbling over an open fire.

And sure enough, there were nine more fat,
merry little rabbits hopping around it!
When they saw the fish, they popped them into
the stew, along with the mushrooms and herbs.
The stew began to smell very good indeed.

And when they saw the tawny, scrawny lion, they gave him a big bowl of hot stew. And then they hopped about so busily, that really, it would have been quite a job for that tired, hungry lion to catch even one of them!

So he gobbled his stew, but the rabbits filled his bowl again. When he had eaten all he could hold, they heaped his bowl with berries.

And when the berries were gone—the
tawny, scrawny lion wasn't scrawny any more!
He felt so good and fat and comfortable that
he couldn't even move.

"Here's a fine thing!" he said to himself.
"All these fat little rabbits, and I haven't room
inside for even one!"
He looked at all those fine, fat little rabbits
and wished he'd get hungry again.

"Mind if I stay a while?" he asked.
"We wouldn't even hear of your going!"
said the rabbits. Then they plumped
themselves down in the lion's lap and began
to sing songs.

And somehow, even when it was time to say
goodnight, that lion wasn't one bit hungry!
 Home he went, through the soft moonlight,
singing softly to himself. He curled up in his bed,
patted his sleek, fat tummy, and smiled.
 When he woke up in the morning, it was Monday.
 "Time to chase monkeys!" said the lion.

But he wasn't one bit hungry for monkeys!
What he wanted was some more of that tasty
carrot stew. So off he went to visit the rabbits.

On Tuesday he didn't want kangaroos, and
on Wednesday he didn't want zebras. He wasn't
hungry for bears on Thursday, or camels on
Friday, or elephants on Saturday.

All the big animals were so surprised and happy!

They dressed in their best and went to see the fat little rabbit.

"Rabbit," they said. "Oh, you wonderful rabbit! What in the world did you talk to the tawny, scrawny, hungry, terrible lion about?"

The fat little rabbit jumped up in the air and said, "Oh, my goodness! We had such a good time with that nice, jolly lion that I guess we forgot to talk about anything at all!"

And before the big animals could say one word, the tawny lion came skipping up the path. He had a basket of berries for the fat rabbit sisters, and a string of fish for the fat rabbit brothers, and a big bunch of daisies for the fat rabbit himself. "I came for supper," he said, shaking paws all around.

Then he sat down in the soft grass, looking
fat as butter, sleek as satin, and jolly as all get
out, all ready for another good big supper of
carrot stew.

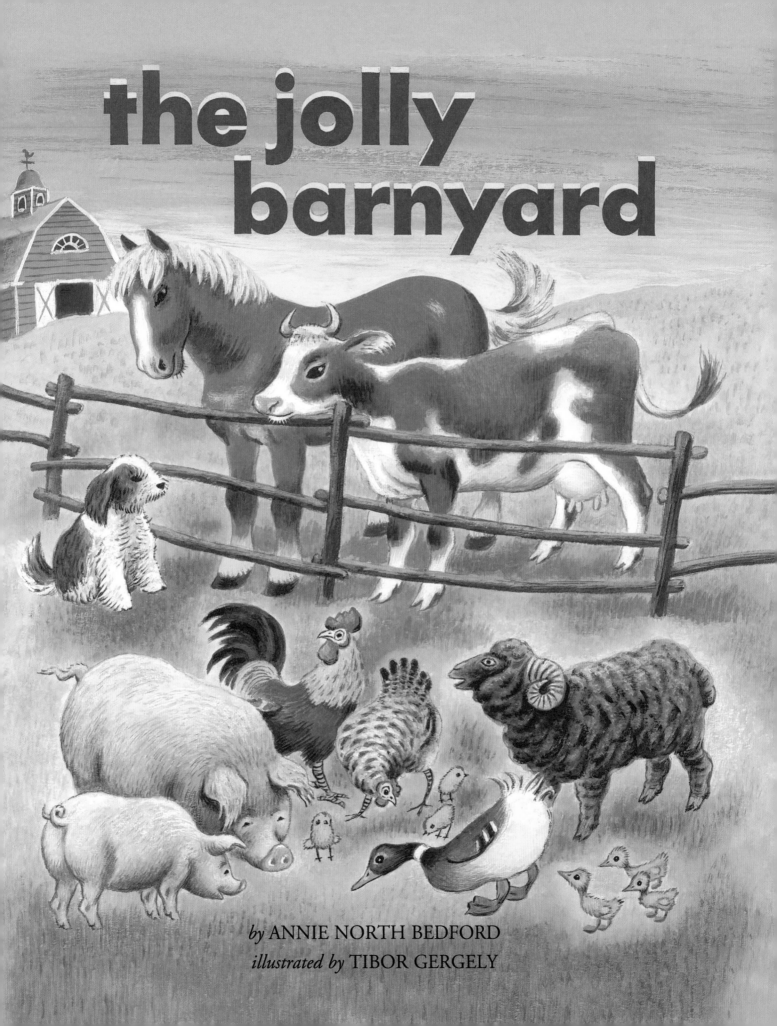

the jolly barnyard

by ANNIE NORTH BEDFORD

illustrated by TIBOR GERGELY

Said Farmer Brown, "Tra-la, tra-lee!
Today is my birthday, lucky me!
I'll give my animals a treat—
for each, what he likes best to eat."

First he took a pan of oats, of course,
to the baby colt and the mother horse.

For the cow and calf he set corn down.
"'Cause today is my birthday," said Farmer Brown.

The big white ram and the fat black sheep
ate all the grain in a great big heap.

The gobbling turkey ate and ate until
he had to admit he'd eaten his fill.

The chickens and rooster got their food—
enough for all their hungry brood.

And so did the duck, and so did the drake
and the ducklings down beside the lake.

The dog got bones to bury and to chew.

The cat got milk—and the kitten did, too.

When all the animals had been fed,
Farmer Brown left, and the spotted cow said:

"Kind Farmer Brown! What would you say
we could do for him on his birthday?"

"We'll pull his loads smoothly, with never a jolt,"
said the big brown horse and her little brown colt.

"Moo-oo, I'll give him lots of milk," said the cow.
Said her calf, "I will, too, someday, somehow!"

"Baa-aa, we'll give him wool," said the sheep.
"For our fleece is soft and warm and deep."

"Gobble!" said the turkey. "As well as I am able,
I'll decorate his Thanksgiving table."

"Cluck! I will give him eggs," said the hen.
Said the rooster, "I'll wake him in the
mornings, then."

"Quack! He can have duck eggs," said the duck.
"And I'll swim on his pond," said the drake,
"for luck."

"Bow-wow!" said the dog. "I'll guard his house
both night and day, but most of all when
he's away!"

"Mew! We'll catch his mice," said the cat.
"We're good hunters," said the kitten.
"Farmer Brown will tell you that."

Inside the farmhouse was another treat—
a beautiful birthday cake to eat.
What a happy birthday for Farmer Brown!

TOOTLE

by GERTRUDE CRAMPTON

illustrated by TIBOR GERGELY

Far, far to the west of everywhere is the village of Lower Trainswitch. All the baby locomotives go there to learn to be big locomotives. The young locomotives steam up and down the tracks, trying to call out the long, sad *ToooOoooot* of the big locomotives. But the best they can do is a gay little *Tootle.*

Lower Trainswitch has a fine school for engines. There are lessons in Whistle Blowing, Stopping for a Red Flag Waving, Puffing Loudly When Starting, Coming Around Curves Safely, Screeching When Stopping, and Clicking and Clacking Over the Rails.

Of all the things that are taught in the
Lower Trainswitch School for Locomotives,
the most important is, of course, Staying on
the Rails No Matter What.

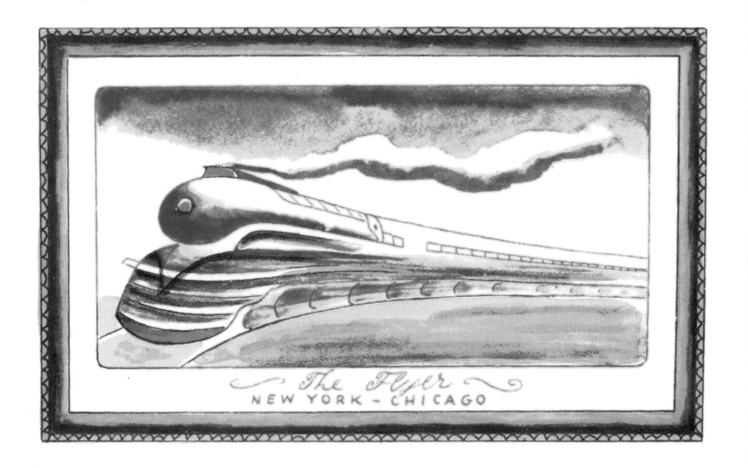

The Flyer
NEW YORK – CHICAGO

The head of the school is an old engineer named Bill. Bill always tells the new locomotives that he will not be angry if they sometimes spill the soup pulling the diner, or if they turn the milk to butter now and then. But they will never, never be good trains unless they get 100 A+ in Staying on the Rails No Matter What. All the baby engines work very hard to get 100 A+ in Staying on the Rails. After a few weeks not one of the engines in the Lower Trainswitch School for Trains would even think of getting off the rails, no matter—well, no matter what.

One day a new locomotive named Tootle came to school.

"Here is the finest baby I've seen since old 600," thought Bill. He patted the gleaming young locomotive and said, "How would you like to grow up to be the Flyer between New York and Chicago?"

"If a Flyer goes very fast, I should like to be one," Tootle answered. "I love to go fast. Watch me."

He raced all around the roundhouse.
"Good! Good!" said Bill. "You must study
Whistle Blowing, Puffing Loudly When
Starting, Stopping for a Red Flag Waving, and
Pulling the Diner without Spilling the Soup.

"But most of all you must study Staying on the Rails No Matter What. Remember, you can't be a Flyer unless you get 100 A+ in Staying on the Rails."

Tootle promised that he would remember and that he would work very hard.

He did, too.

He even worked hard at Stopping for a Red Flag Waving. Tootle did not like those lessons at all. There is nothing a locomotive hates more than stopping.

But Bill said that no locomotive ever, ever kept going when he saw a red flag waving.

One day, while Tootle was practicing for his lesson in Staying on the Rails No Matter What, a dreadful thing happened.

He looked across the meadow he was running through and saw a fine, strong black horse.

"Race you to the river," shouted the black horse, and kicked up his heels.

Away went the horse. His black tail streamed out behind him, and his mane tossed in the wind. Oh, how he could run!

"Here I go," said Tootle to himself.

"If I am going to be a Flyer, I can't let a horse beat me," he puffed. "Everyone at school will laugh at me."

His wheels turned so fast that they were silver streaks. The cars lurched and bumped together. And just as Tootle was sure he could win, the tracks made a great curve.

"Oh, Whistle!" cried Tootle. "That horse will beat me now. He'll run straight while I take the Great Curve."

Then the Dreadful Thing happened. After all that Bill had said about Staying on the Rails No Matter What, Tootle jumped off the tracks and raced alongside the black horse!

The race ended in a tie. Both Tootle and the black horse were happy. They stood on the bank of the river and talked.

"It's nice here in the meadow," Tootle said.

When Tootle got back to school, he said nothing about leaving the rails. But he thought about it that night in the roundhouse.

"Tomorrow I will work hard," decided
Tootle. "I will not even think of leaving the
rails, no matter what."

And he did work hard. He practiced
tootling so much that the Mayor Himself
ran up the hill, his green coattails flapping,
and said that everyone in the village had
a headache and would he please stop
TOOTLING.

So Tootle was sent to practice Staying on
the Rails No Matter What.

As he came to the Great Curve, Tootle looked across the meadow. It was full of buttercups.

"It's like a big yellow carpet. How I should like to play in them and hold one under my searchlight to see if I like butter!" thought Tootle. "But no, I am going to be a Flyer and I must practice Staying on the Rails No Matter What!"

Tootle clicked and clacked around the Great Curve. His wheels began to say over and over again, "Do you like butter? Do you?"

"I don't know," said Tootle crossly. "But I'm going to find out."

He stopped much faster than any good Flyer ever does, unless he is stopping for a Red Flag Waving. He hopped off the tracks and bumped along the meadow to the yellow buttercups.

"What fun!" said Tootle.

And he danced around and around and held one of the buttercups under his searchlight.

"I do like butter!" cried Tootle. "I do!"

At last the sun began to go down, and it was time to hurry to the roundhouse.

That evening while the Chief Oiler was playing checkers with old Bill, he said, "It's queer. It's very queer, but I found grass between Tootle's front wheels today."

"Hmm," said Bill. "There must be grass growing on the tracks."

"Not on our tracks," said the Day Watchman, who spent his days watching the tracks and his nights watching Bill and the Chief Oiler play checkers.

Bill's face was stern. "Tootle knows he must get 100 A+ in Staying on the Rails No Matter What, if he is going to be a Flyer."

Next day Tootle played all day in the meadow. He watched a green frog and he made a daisy chain. He found a rain barrel, and he said softly, "Toot!" "TOOT!" shouted the barrel. "Why, I sound like a Flyer already!" cried Tootle.

That night the First Assistant Oiler said he
had found a daisy in Tootle's bell. The day
after that, the Second Assistant Oiler said that
he had found hollyhock flowers floating in
Tootle's eight bowls of soup.

And then the Mayor Himself said that he had seen Tootle chasing butterflies in the meadow. The Mayor Himself said that Tootle had looked very silly, too.

Early one morning Bill had a long, long talk with the Mayor Himself.

When the Mayor Himself left the Lower Trainswitch School for Locomotives, he laughed all the way to the village.

"Bill's plan will surely put Tootle back on the track," he chuckled.

Bill ran from one store to the next, buying ten yards of this and twenty yards of that and all you have of the other. The Chief Oiler and the First, Second, and Third Assistant Oilers were hammering and sawing instead of oiling and polishing. And Tootle? Well, Tootle was in the meadow watching the butterflies flying and wishing he could dip and soar as they did.

Not a store in Lower Trainswitch was open the next day and not a person was at home. By the time the sun came up, every villager was hiding in the meadow along the tracks. And each of them had a red flag. It had taken all the red goods in Lower Trainswitch, and hard work by the Oilers, but there was a red flag for everyone.

Soon Tootle came tootling happily down the tracks. When he came to the meadow, he hopped off the tracks and rolled along the grass. Just as he was thinking what a beautiful day it was, a red flag poked up from the grass and waved hard. Tootle stopped, for every locomotive knows he must Stop for a Red Flag Waving.

"I'll go another way," said Tootle.

He turned to the left, and up came another waving red flag, this time from the middle of the buttercups.

When he went to the right, there was another red flag waving.

There were red flags waving from the buttercups, in the daisies, under the trees, near the bluebirds' nest, and even one behind the rain barrel. And, of course, Tootle had to stop for each one, for a locomotive must always Stop for a Red Flag Waving.

"Red flags," muttered Tootle. "This meadow is full of red flags. How can I have any fun?

"Whenever I start, I have to stop. Why did
I think this meadow was such a fine place?
Why don't I ever see a green flag?"

Just as the tears were ready to slide out of
his boiler, Tootle happened to look back over
his coal car. On the tracks stood Bill, and
in his hand was a big green flag. "Oh!" said
Tootle.

He puffed up to Bill and stopped.

"This is the place for me," said Tootle.
"There is nothing but red flags for
locomotives that get off their tracks."

"Hurray!" shouted the people of Lower
Trainswitch, and jumped up from their hiding
places. "Hurray for Tootle the Flyer!"

Now Tootle is a famous Two-Miles-a-Minute
Flyer. The young locomotives listen to his advice.
"Work hard," he tells them. "Always remember
to Stop for a Red Flag Waving. But most of all,
Stay on the Rails No Matter What."